Chimpanzees!

An Animal Encyclopedia for Kids (Monkey Kingdom)

Children's Biological Science of Apes & Monkeys Books

PROFESSOR GUSTO

EDUCATIONAL & INFORMATIVE BOOKS FOR CHILDREN
(PRE-K / K-12)

HEY KIDS, DO YOU WANT TO LEARN AMAZING FACTS ABOUT CHIMPANZEES?

ARE THEY MONKEYS? NO. THEY BELONG TO THE APE FAMILY.

ARE THEY RELATED TO US?
YES, AND THEY ARE ALSO
RELATED TO GORILLAS
AND ORANGUTANS.

CHIMPS CAN BE YOUR FRIENDS!

Chimpanzees are known as our closest relatives.

These primates are usually found in Africa, particularly in the grassland, rainforest and woodland of West and Central Africa. Long dark hair covers their bodies.

But, unlike monkeys, chimpanzees have no tails. Unfortunately, these animals are considered endangered.

WHAT CAUSED THE REDUCTION OF THEIR POPULATION?

They lost their habitat due to commercial hunting.

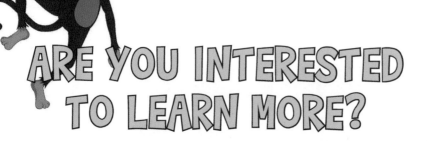

ARE YOU INTERESTED TO LEARN MORE?

Chimpanzees are omnivores. They eat both plants and animals. They eat fruits, insects, and meat.

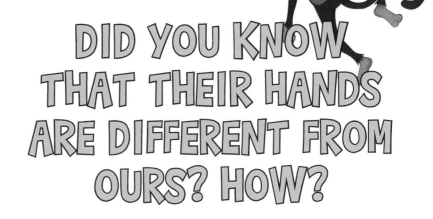

DID YOU KNOW THAT THEIR HANDS ARE DIFFERENT FROM OURS? HOW?

Their thumb is not in the same line with their other fingers.

It is in opposition with the other four fingers. This would allow them to groom each other and to use tools.

They are one of the most intelligent primates on Earth. They use tools to get ants from holes in trees and they use stones to break nuts.

Chimpanzees get sick too, just like humans. They can be infected with diseases like Hepatitis B, influenza, measles and many others.

They communicate with others by using sounds and gestures. They even exchange hugs and kisses. When they get sick, they usually heal themselves by eating medicinal plants.

DO THEY KEEP THEMSELVES CLEAN?

Yes, definitely. Grooming is their ritual, which develops close relationships between community members.

HOW DO THEY SPEND THEIR LEISURE OR FREE TIME?

If they are bored, they usually have games for entertainment. They are observed to laugh while playing with others.

WHERE DO CHIMPANZEES SLEEP?

Chimpanzees sleep in the trees. They build their nests in the trees and they usually spend their nights there. But, every night, a chimpanzee always changes the location of his nest.

HOW DO THEY WALK?

Chimpanzees have four limbs for walking but they can also walk on two legs or hind legs.

HOW ABOUT THEIR REPRODUCTION AND BABIES?

Female chimpanzees will produce a baby once every 5 or 6 years. Bonding between the mother and the baby will last for over 7 years.

Their babies have a white tail that will disappear in time. When female chimpanzees get pregnant, it'll take between 8 and 9 months for a baby chimp to be born.

First-time moms observe other mother chimpanzees on how to take care of the baby. According to biology, the chimpanzee's **DNA** is closer to humans than that of the gorilla's.

DID YOU KNOW THAT 96 PERCENT OF OUR DNA IS FOUND IN THE CHIMPANZEES?

Chimpanzees have a life span of 40-50 years when they are in the wild, but in captivity they can reach 50-60 years.

Chimpanzees are social animals. They usually socialize through kissing, tickling and hugging.

These animals share their food with other chimps. They even take care of babies which are not theirs biologically.

Male chimpanzees stay in the community while the females usually venture out in other communities.

Did you know that the skin of chimpanzees gets darker as they grow older? Yes, that's true.

Their most dangerous
predators are the leopards.

WOULD YOU LIKE TO MEET SOME CHIMPS?

ASK YOUR PARENTS TO TAKE YOU TO THE ZOO TO SEE THEM!

Printed in Great Britain
by Amazon

17556544R00025